Emmy
the Exaggerating Elephant
Fenton
the Fearful Frog
Gertie
the Grungy Goat
Herbie
the Happy Hamster
Ivy
the Impatient Iguana
Rupert
the Resourceful Rhinoceros
Ollie
the Obedient Ostrich
Perry
the Polite Porcupine
Queenie
the Quiet Quail
Ziggy
the Zippy Zebra
Yori
the Yucky Yak
Xavier
the X-ploring Xenops
Wendy
the Wise Woodchuck
D1120117

NOTE TO PARENTS

Katy's Surprise
A story about kindness

Katy the Kind Koala enjoys helping others. She spends some part of every day doing something thoughtful or helpful for her AlphaPet friends and neighbors. Sometimes she even helps her friends when it's least convenient for her. When Katy has an accident, she learns that her many kindnesses are not forgotten.

In addition to enjoying this inspiring story with your child, you can use it to teach a gentle lesson about the importance of being kind and thoughtful. Discuss the meaning of the golden rule and the saying, "What goes around, comes around." Explain that when someone is kind to others, others will usually be kind in return.

You can also use this story to introduce the letter **K**. As you read about Katy the Kind Koala, ask your child to listen for all the words that start with **K** and point to the objects that begin with **K**. (Your child might choose words that begin with the hard C sound, since they sound alike.) When you've finished reading the story, your child will enjoy doing the activity at the end of the book.

The AlphaPets™ characters were conceived and created by Ruth Lerner Perle.
Characters interpreted and designed by Deborah Colvin Borgo.
Cover/book design and production by Norton & Company.
Logo design by Deborah Colvin Borgo and Nancy S. Norton.
Grolier Books is a Division of Grolier Enterprises, Inc. Printed and Manufactured in the United States of America

Katy's Surprise

RUTH LERNER PERLE
Illustrated by Judy Blankenship

Katy the Kind Koala spends most of her afternoons visiting her AlphaPet friends and neighbors. Sometimes she has a nice friendly chat with them, sometimes she brings them things they need, and sometimes she lends them a helping hand.

In the mornings, when the weather is good, Katy loves to run through the meadow flying her big red kite.

One morning, when Katy was flying her kite, Nelly the Naughty Newt came running over to her.

"That's a great kite!" shouted Nelly. "I want to fly it!" Nelly grabbed Katy's kite and started to run. Katy ran after her.

"Hey, Nelly. That's not nice! You didn't have to grab my kite. I'd be glad to let you fly it," Katy said when she caught up with Nelly. "I have to go now, anyway. I promised to help Lizzy in her garden. Have fun with my kite, but please be sure to return it to me this afternoon."

Nelly ran off with the kite, and Katy went to visit Lizzy the Lazy Lamb.

When Katy arrived at Lizzy's house, Lizzy was leaning peacefully against her garden wall. She opened her eyes and smiled up at Katy. "Hello, there, Katy. It's such a beautiful day," she said. "Come sit by me and we'll take a nice snooze in the sun."

Katy looked at Lizzy's vegetable garden. It was overgrown with weeds. "This is a perfect day to weed your garden," she suggested. "I'd be glad to help you, and then we can have a nice rest when we're finished."

Katy helped Lizzy to her feet and together they weeded the rows of carrots, onions, spinach and kale.

When all the weeds were pulled, Lizzy looked at the neat rows of vegetables. "Oh, Katy," Lizzy said. "I could never have done all that work without your help. Thank you so very much." Lizzy gave Katy a great big kiss. Then they sat down to rest.

After a while, Katy got up and said, "I'd better hurry home now. I want to be there when Nelly comes to return my kite."

But Nelly did not return the kite.

The next morning, Katy said to herself, “Where’s Nelly with my kite? I really hope she gets here soon.”

Katy went down to her kitchen and took a big kettle from the shelf. “I guess I’ll make some chicken soup while I wait for Nelly. Then I’ll have something to offer my friends when they come by,” she said to herself.

Before long, Herbie the Happy Hamster came to visit. Herbie watched as Katy stirred the soup in her big kettle.

"Mmm, that soup sure smells good," Herbie said. "I know how to paint and fix things, but I'm not a very good cook."

"This soup is just about finished," Katy said. "I'd be glad to give you some to take home."

Katy filled some jars with soup and put them in a bag for Herbie.

Herbie took the jars. "You're such a good friend," he said. "Thank you for sharing." Herbie threw Katy a kiss and went on his way.

That afternoon, Katy went to visit Una the Unhappy Unicorn. Una was in her bedroom looking sadly into the mirror.

"Hello, Katy, dear," Una said, wiping her tears. "I wanted to look especially nice for you today, but my hair keeps falling in my face. I wish I could make my hair look pretty."

"Maybe I can help you," said Katy.

Katy combed and brushed Una's hair, and put it up in big pink rollers.

When Una's hair was all combed out, Katy tied a pretty bow in it. "Oh, Katy, my hair looks wonderful," Una said. "You're such a good friend. Thank you. Thank you." Una gave Katy a great big kiss.

When Katy came home, her kite was still not there. "Nelly must really be having fun with my kite. I won't ask for it back just yet, but I do hope she returns it soon," Katy said to herself.

All the next week, Katy continued to help her friends.

On Monday . . .

Katy helped Wendy the Wise Woodchuck return books to the library.

On Tuesday . . .

Katy helped Tina the Truthful Tiger repair her buggy.

On Wednesday . . .

Katy brought Albert the Absentminded Alligator a cutting of her very best plant.

On Thursday . . .

Katy helped Vinnie the Vocal Vulture record his favorite stories.

On Friday . . .

Katy brought Perry the Polite Porcupine a gift of writing paper for his birthday.

On Saturday . . .

Katy helped Queenie the Quiet Quail finish her quilting.

Then, on Sunday,

Yori the Yucky Yak said, “I need someone to take care of my spiders and worms while I paint their box. Will you babysit for them? They’re so cute and they tickle when they crawl on your arms.”

“Well, er, ah, that is . . . I guess . . . I’ll try my best, Yori. But please paint the box as fast as you can,” said Katy.

Katy did not like spiders or other creepy crawly things but she did want to help her friend, so she agreed.

More than a week had gone by, but Nelly had still not returned the kite.

A few days later, Katy and Bradley the Brave Bear were walking in the meadow. "The breeze is perfect for kite-flying today! How I wish I had my kite," said Katy.

"Then why don't you tell Nelly to return your kite?" Bradley asked.

"Well," Katy said, "Nelly doesn't have a kite of her own. Even though I want my kite back, it makes me feel good that I can help her be happy. I'm always glad to share my things."

Bradley and Katy walked along. Suddenly, in the distance, Katy saw Nelly with her kite! Katy ran toward her. But as she ran, kerplunk!, Katy stumbled on a tree stump and fell.

"My foot, my foot!" Katy cried. "Oh, I really hurt my foot!"

Bradley ran for help. And soon they were in the hospital.

The doctor examined Katy's foot. "The muscles are badly strained," he said. "You need lots of rest . . . and don't put any weight on that foot. Don't worry, in a few weeks you'll be as good as new."

Get
WeLL
SOON

Well! When the AlphaPets heard what had happened, they all agreed to pitch in and help take care of their dear friend. When Katy came home,

Lizzy brought fresh vegetables from her garden.

Una came to fix Katy's hair every day.

Queenie brought her quilt to keep Katy warm.

Wendy brought her books to read.

Herbie came with a jar of Katy's own chicken soup.

Albert brought a flower that he cut from his plant.

Tina offered to drive Katy wherever she wanted to go.

Perry wrote a cheery get-well message every day.

AND, *yuck!* Yori brought his spiders and worms for visits!

Then Vinnie stepped forward and everyone quieted down to hear what he would say.

"Dearest friends," he started, "I must take this opportunity to say a few words—just a very few words—about our dear, dear, Katy: Katy the Kind Koala. As we all know, Katy has a heart of gold. Yes, indeed. For a long time now, she has been helping us out whenever we needed her. It is said, 'Do unto others as you would have them do unto you.' Oh, yes. And, 'What goes around, comes around.'

"Now that Katy needs us, we are here by her side ready to do what we can for her. I believe I can say, and I'm sure you will all agree, that life in AlphaPet Corners would not be the cheery place it is if it weren't for our Katy's kindness. We wish her a speedy recovery!"

Everyone smiled and clapped, including Lizzy, who had just awoken from a short nap.

Una
XXOO
Tina

Katy sat up on her pillows. As she was about to thank everyone, she noticed something red flapping outside her window. It was her kite! Nelly had come to return it at last. There was a long yellow streamer tied to the kite's tail that said: Many Thanks Katy—Get Well Soon! Your friend, Nelly.

Nelly felt proud and happy, and Katy's foot felt much better, too.

Kindly learn these words with me.

kettle

kilt

kitchen

kayak

Look back at the pictures in this book and try to find these and other things that begin with the letter K.

Aa Bb

Gg Hh

Mm Nn Oo Pp

Uu Vv Ww